OAKLAND RAIDERS

BY BRIAN HOWELL

The Child's World®

Published by The Child's World®
1980 Lookout Drive • Mankato, MN 56003-1705
800-599-READ • www.childsworld.com

Acknowledgments
The Child's World®: Mary Berendes, Publishing Director
Red Line Editorial: Editorial direction
The Design Lab: Design
Amnet: Production

Design Element: Dean Bertoncelj/Shutterstock Images
Photographs ©: Marcio Jose Sanchez/AP Images, cover;
John McDonough/SI/Icon Sportswire, 5; Al Golub/AP
Images, 7; ZumaPress/Icon Sportswire, 9; Ben Margot/
AP Images, 11; Shutterstock Images, 13; Rich Pedroncelli/
AP Images, 14–15; AP Images, 17; Elise Amendola/AP
Images, 19; Greg Trott/AP Images, 21; Lennox McLendon/
AP Images, 23; Daniel Gluskoter/Icon Sportswire, 25; Ric
Tapia/AP Images, 27; NFL/AP Images, 29

ISBN 9781634070010
LCCN 2014959705

Printed in the United States of America
Mankato, MN
July, 2015
PA02265

ABOUT THE AUTHOR

Brian Howell is a freelance writer based in Denver, Colorado. He has been a sports journalist for nearly 20 years and has written dozens of books about sports and two about American history. A native of Colorado, he lives with his wife and four children in his home state.

TABLE OF CONTENTS

GO, RAIDERS!

The Oakland Raiders have played in the **Super Bowl** five times. Only a few teams have played in more. The Raiders won three of those. The team has had some famous players. It also had famous coach John Madden. He led the team to success. Oakland fans are a colorful bunch. They stick by their team even in bad times. Let's meet the Raiders.

Wide receiver Tim Brown has more career touchdowns, receptions, and receiving yards than any other Raiders player.

WHO ARE THE RAIDERS?

The Oakland Raiders play in the National Football **League** (NFL). They are one of the 32 teams in the NFL. The NFL includes the American Football Conference (AFC) and the National Football Conference (NFC). The winner of the AFC plays the winner of the NFC in the Super Bowl. The Raiders play in the West Division of the AFC. They won the Super Bowl after the 1976, 1980, and 1983 seasons.

Running back Bo Jackson, who played professional football and baseball, was with the Raiders from 1987 to 1990.

WHERE THEY CAME FROM

A new professional football league started in 1960. It was called the American Football League (AFL). The Raiders were one of its eight teams. The AFL ended after the 1969 season. So the Raiders joined the NFL. They played in Oakland from 1960 to 1981. Team owner Al Davis moved the team to Los Angeles in 1982. The Raiders stayed there for 13 seasons. But they moved back to Oakland in 1995.

Al Davis (left) coached the Raiders from 1963 to 1965 before becoming owner.

WHO THEY PLAY

The Oakland Raiders play 16 games each season. With so few games, each one is important. Every year, the Raiders play two games against each of the other three teams in their division. Those teams are the Denver Broncos, Kansas City Chiefs, and San Diego Chargers. The Raiders also play six other teams from the AFC and four from the NFC. The Broncos, Chiefs, Raiders, and Chargers all played in the AFL West, too. The Raiders and Chiefs are big **rivals**.

Oakland and the Kansas City Chiefs have been playing memorable games against each other for more than 50 years.

WHERE THEY PLAY

The Raiders had three homes from 1960 to 1965. The Oakland-Alameda County Coliseum opened in 1966. It is now known as O.co Coliseum. The Raiders played there until 1981. They played in the Los Angeles Memorial Coliseum from 1982 to 1994. Then they moved back to Oakland-Alameda County Coliseum in 1995. O.co Coliseum is still the Raiders' home today. The Oakland Athletics baseball team also plays there.

The Raiders and Oakland Athletics share O.co Coliseum, which sits next to Oracle Arena, home of the Golden State Warriors basketball team.

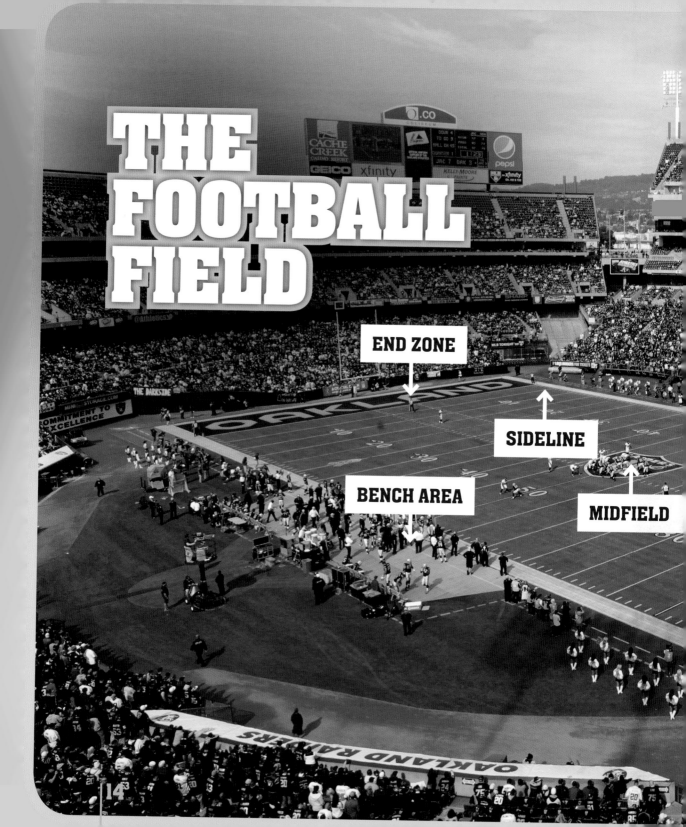

THE FOOTBALL FIELD

END ZONE

SIDELINE

BENCH AREA

MIDFIELD

14

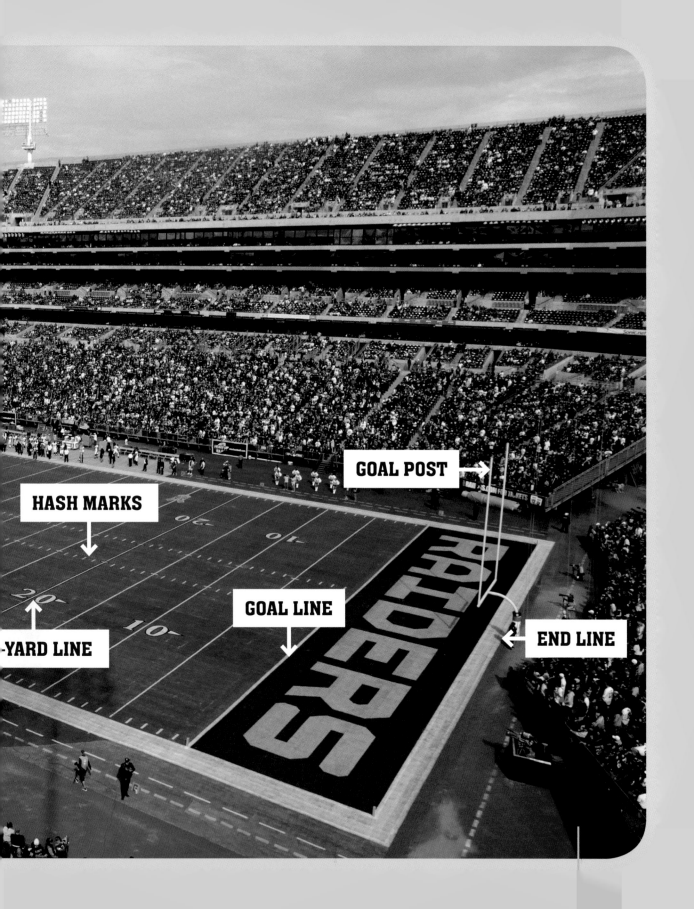

GOAL POST →

HASH MARKS

GOAL LINE

YARD LINE

END LINE

BIG DAYS

The Raiders have had some great moments in their history. Here are three of the greatest:

1969—John Madden was named head coach on February 4. He became one of the best NFL coaches. Madden led the team from 1969 to 1978. The Raiders went 103-32-7 in that time.

1976—This was the Raiders' best season. The team went 16-1 including the **playoffs**. Oakland won its final 13 games. The last was in the Super Bowl on January 9, 1977. The Raiders beat the Minnesota Vikings 32-14.

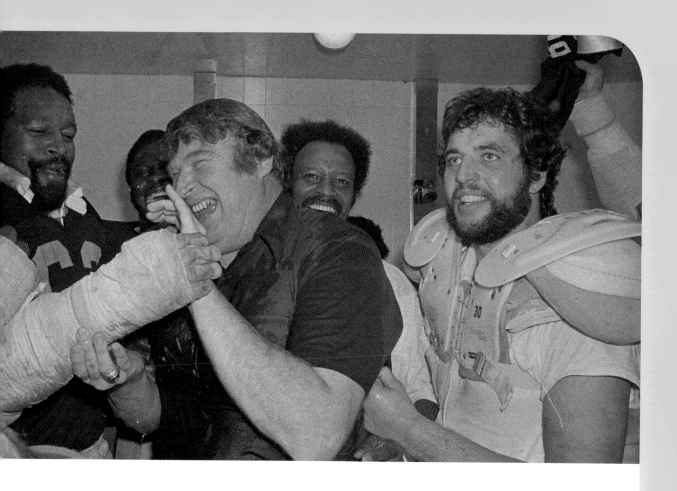

Coach John Madden (middle) led the Raiders to their first Super Bowl title after the 1976 season.

1983—The Raiders won the team's third Super Bowl in eight seasons. They beat the Washington Redskins 38-9 on January 22, 1984. Running back Marcus Allen dominated. He rushed for 191 yards and two **touchdowns**. Allen was named **Most Valuable Player (MVP)** of the game.

TOUGH DAYS

Football is a hard game. Even the best teams have rough games and seasons. Here are some of the toughest times in Raiders history:

1962—The Raiders' third season was one of their worst. They went 1-13 and scored the fewest points in the AFL.

2002—The 2001 Raiders were in the playoffs. They played the New England Patriots on January 19. It was snowing. Cornerback Charles Woodson **sacked** Patriots quarterback Tom Brady. Brady fumbled. But the referee said Brady was tucking away the ball when Woodson hit him. So New England kept possession. The Patriots won in **overtime**. It became known as "The Tuck Rule Game."

"The Tuck Rule Game" is one of the worst moments in Raiders history.

2005—Quarterback Rich Gannon was the NFL MVP in 2002. He led the Raiders to that season's Super Bowl. But he injured his shoulder in 2003. Then he injured his neck in 2004. He retired on August 6.

MEET THE FANS

Raiders fans are known as "Raider Nation." The loudest section of fans is called "The Black Hole." Those fans dress up in crazy silver and black costumes. Their outfits include skulls, spikes, and face paint. "The Black Hole" tries to intimidate other teams. It can be scary to look up at the screaming fans.

Running back Marcel Reese celebrates with fans in "The Black Hole" after a win over the Buffalo Bills on December 21, 2014.

HEROES THEN

Quarterback Ken Stabler led Oakland to its first Super Bowl win. He was the NFL MVP in 1974. Running back Marcus Allen was named MVP in 1985. And quarterback Rich Gannon won the award in 2002. Offensive linemen Art Shell and Gene Upshaw played together from 1968 to 1981. They are both in the Pro Football Hall of Fame. Defensive lineman Howie Long is a legend. Tim Brown is the best Raiders wide receiver ever. He had 14,934 receiving yards. That was second-most in NFL history when he retired in 2005.

Running back Marcus Allen (top) led the NFL with 1,759 rushing yards in his 1985 MVP season.

HEROES NOW

Defensive back Charles Woodson played for Oakland from 1998 to 2005. He then returned in 2013. He helps lead the defense. Oakland drafted quarterback Derek Carr in 2014. He started the first game that season. No other Raiders rookie quarterback had done that. The Raiders chose kicker Sebastian Janikowski in the first round of the 2000 NFL Draft. He was the first kicker to make two field goals of at least 60 yards.

Quarterback Derek Carr set rookie quarterback records for the Raiders in 2014.

GEARING UP

NFL players wear team uniforms. They wear helmets and pads to keep them safe. Cleats help them make quick moves and run fast. Some players wear extra gear for protection.

THE FOOTBALL

NFL footballs are made of leather. Under the leather is a lining that fills with air to give the ball its shape. The leather has bumps or "pebbles." These help players grip the ball. Laces help players control their throws. Footballs are also called "pigskins" because some of the first balls were made from pig bladders. Today they are made of leather from cows.

Defensive back Charles Woodson made the Pro Bowl in his first four NFL seasons.

HELMET

SHOULDER PADS

LOVES

THIG PADS

FOOTBALL

27

SPORTS STATS

ere are some of the all-time career records for the Oakland Raiders. All the stats are through the 2014 season.

INTERCEPTIONS

Willie Brown 39

Lester Hayes 39

RUSHING YARDS

Marcus Allen 8,545

Mark van Eeghen 5,907

RECEPTIONS

Tim Brown 1,070

Fred Biletnikoff 589

TOTAL TOUCHDOWNS

Tim Brown 104

Marcus Allen 98

SACKS

Greg Townsend 107.5

Howie Long 84

POINTS

Sebastian Janikowski 1,574

George Blanda 863

Quarterback Ken Stabler led the Raiders to their first Super Bowl victory.

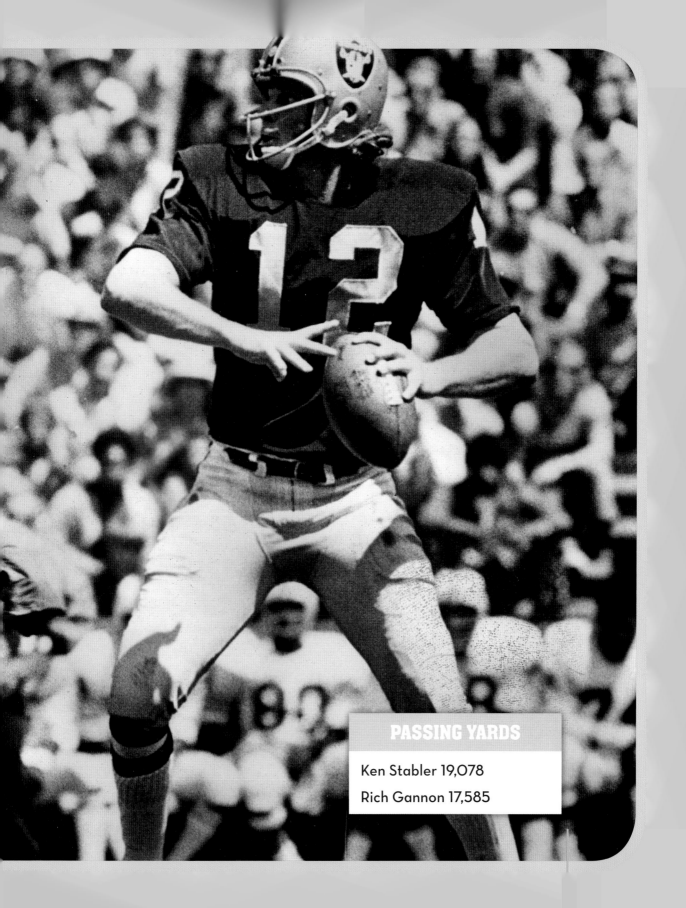

PASSING YARDS

Ken Stabler 19,078

Rich Gannon 17,585

GLOSSARY

league an organization of sports teams that compete against each other

Most Valuable Player (MVP) a yearly award given to the top player in the NFL

overtime extra time that is played when teams are tied at the end of four quarters

playoffs a series of games after the regular season that decides which two teams play in the Super Bowl

rivals teams whose games bring out the greatest emotion between the players and the fans on both sides

sacked when a quarterback is tackled behind the line of scrimmage before he can throw the ball

Super Bowl the championship game of the NFL, played between the winners of the AFC and the NFC

touchdowns plays in which the ball is held in the other team's end zone, resulting in six points

FIND OUT MORE

IN THE LIBRARY

Flores, Tom, and Matt Fulks. *Tales from the Oakland Raiders Sideline*. New York: Skyhorse Publishing, 2012.

Frisch, Nate. *The Story of the Oakland Raiders*. Mankato, MN: Creative Education, 2014.

Gutierrez, Paul. *100 Things Raiders Fans Should Know & Do Before They Die*. Chicago: Triumph Books, 2014.

ON THE WEB

Visit our Web site for links about the Oakland Raiders:
childsworld.com/links

Note to Parents, Teachers, and Librarians: We routinely verify our Web links to make sure they are safe and active sites. So encourage your readers to check them out!

INDEX